Dedicated to:
Grandma Bernie, possibly the most patient woman in the world. You've taught me more about being gentle in this world than I could possibly say. Hoot!

My Mama, Jolene, who has been enthusiastically supportive in all of my crazy endeavors.
I am forever grateful for you.

A Hoot in the Storm

Written by Mary Runkel, illustrated by Chana de Moura.

"A Hoot in the Storm" is a woman-empowerment project. Thanks to the editors, readers and encouragers for helping make this book a reality. Special thanks to Kelsea Graham for the graphic design work.

ISBN: 978-0-578-64383-0

Library of Congress Cataloging-in-publication data is available. Printed in Denver, Colorado in the United States of America. First edition: June 2020.

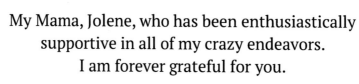

A Hoot in the Storm

A Story of Two Night Owls

Written by Mary Runkel
Illustrated by Chana de Moura

I am a tiny, feathery, hooting owl.
My name is Little Hoot but when
hoomans see me, they call me "barred."

I live in a great, green forest
in a tall and creaky tree.

I love to fly.

I go Quick!   Fast!
Up!
        Around!
Down!

Through the forests and grasses. I can
make it to the creek in less time than
it takes Gram Owl to hoot a full call,

" WHO WHO WHO WHOOOOOOO! "

3

My favorite treats are little mice
I find in the fields near my tree.
They are delicious!

The sun goes down as I travel my forest,
and I often visit Gram Owl's tree.

She lives in a grand, old,
hallowed oak on the
edge of the thicket.

Gram Owl is a master at collecting
things. Her nest is made of shiny
and funny bits of hooman life.

When she shows me her discoveries,
I nod up and down, up and down.
I like them a lot.

Gram Owl teaches me about
the great moon and secret
places to find my favorite mice.

She keeps all her best hiding
places just for me.

10

We stay up later than other owls.
"Little Hoot! My, what time is it?"
She asks. "You better get home
before the sun rises!"

"But Gram Owl," I say. "I'm not even
tired!" And she **winks**—at least I think
it's a wink—and we cuddle and coo
about the critters we caught.

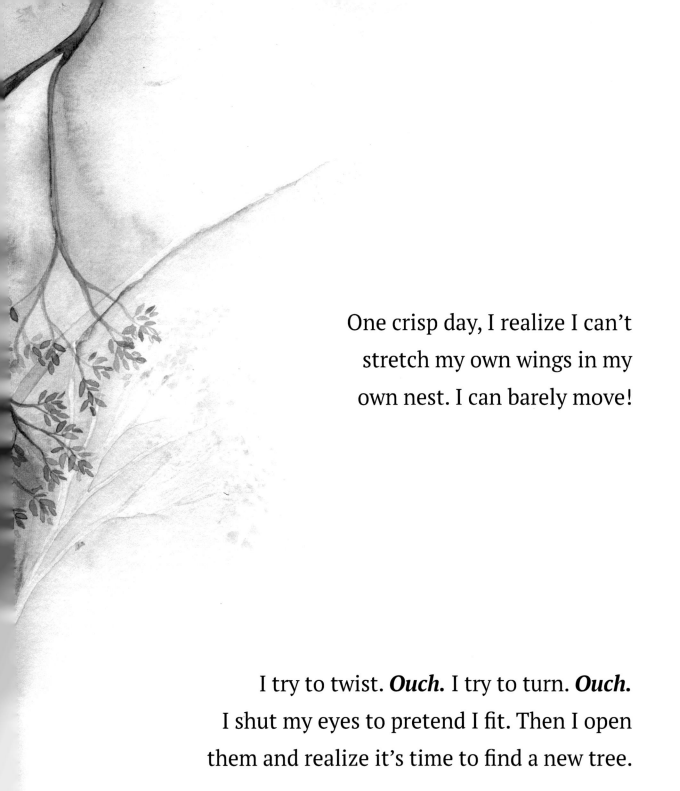

One crisp day, I realize I can't
stretch my own wings in my
own nest. I can barely move!

I try to twist. **Ouch.** I try to turn. **Ouch.**
I shut my eyes to pretend I fit. Then I open
them and realize it's time to find a new tree.

I search around the
forest. I check with
the squirrels. I don't
find a suitable tree.

They're too small.
Too twiggy. So I
keep searching.

Then, one day when I take the long route, I find it. The perfect tree. My wings can stretch. I can see forever. The only problem? It's far, far away.

After a few weeks of roaming
my new hills,
I realize how far I am from
where I once lived.

I love my new tree, but ooooh.
It's FAR away from my great,
green forest.
No one hears me hoot.
No one...including Gram Owl.

So mostly, I stay silent.

Don't cuddle.

Don't coo.

I miss my night route. I miss how
the moon rose over the forest.

But most of all, I miss my early-morning-after-all-
other-owls-have-perched night owl friend.

My Gram Owl, who hoots at the same hours as I do.

I know Gram Owl cannot fly to see me.
She cannot make the trip alone.
Her wings are tired from years
of hunting prey and collecting.

I have never felt so alone.

One very dark eve, a giant storm
moves across the hills. It shakes
my new tree and lights up the others.

The thunder *BOOMS* here and *CRACKS*
there. Will my whole tree fall? Tumble?

I am afraid. I begin to cry,

"Who, who, who!"

And then howl some more.

Then I hear something. Something I know. Something so familiar...

Is it Gram Owl calling me on this very scary night?

Yes, I can hear her
through the wind,
sending me a message!

"Little Hoot," she says.

"Can you be brave? Don't let this scare you, don't be afraid!
Storms are good, they help things grow.
Hang in tight, you're not alone!"

As she calls, I feel less afraid.

I blink my eyes open,

then shut,

shake my feathers

and settle down into my nest.

Tucked away in the hills,
I know my Gram Owl is with me.

And as the sky clears and the sun
comes up, I let out a little "hoot"
to let her know I am with her too.

Made in the USA
Monee, IL
29 November 2020

"Little Hoot, can you be brave?"

Little Hoot visits Gram Owl every night, where they "cuddle and coo" about critters they catch. But one evening, Little Hoot's nest is too small and a new one is on the horizon. Find out how Little Hoot navigates the "storm" of moving away from Gram Owl, familiarity and comfort in this lighthearted story filled with sweet watercolor illustrations.

$14.99
ISBN 978-0-578-64383-0